For Eunice and Maria
with love and thanks
—Emma

First published in hardback
by HarperCollins Publishers USA in 2012

First published in paperback in the UK
by HarperCollins Children's Books in 2012

1 3 5 7 9 10 8 6 4 2

ISBN: 978-0-00-745597-3

HarperCollins Children's Books is a division of HarperCollins Publishers Ltd.

Visit our website at www.harpercollins.co.uk

Printed and bound in China

EMMA DODD

Foxy

HarperCollins *Children's Books*

It was very late. Tomorrow was Monday and Emily would be starting school.

Emily sat up in bed. She looked worried.

"What's the matter?" asked Foxy.
"Whatever it is, I'm sure I can help."

"I'm worried I haven't got all the things I need for my first day at school," said Emily.

Foxy thought he would use his magic tail to help Emily. He waved it back and forth and back and forth so Emily would notice.

"I don't need a tail for school," said Emily. "I need a **pencil**."

Foxy tried again, and this time
he came up with a pencil.
"Now I need a **pencil case**,"
said Emily.

OOPS!

"Thank you, Foxy. I also
have to bring a **notebook**."

"I guess magic is hard," said Emily.

"That's better!"

"I'd love some new **school shoes**," Emily suggested.

"Thank you, Foxy," Emily said politely. "But I think I'll wear my boots to school instead."

"How about a new **hat?**" asked Foxy.

"And here's a **school bag!**"

"No, silly, that's a **pirate flag!**"

$$E = mc^2$$

Emily still looked worried.

"*Now* what's the matter?" asked Foxy.

"What if I am not clever enough?" asked Emily.

Foxy touched Emily with his magic tail.

"Oh dear," said Emily. "I think I would rather learn these things at school."

"And one last thing . . . " said Emily. "What if nobody likes me?"
"Now, you don't need my magic for that, Emily," said Foxy.

"I know you'll make lots of friends."